ABOUT THE BANK STREET READY-TO-READ SERIES

Seventy-five years of educational research and innovative teaching have given the Bank Street College of Education the reputation as America's most trusted name in early childhood education.

Because no two children are exactly alike in their development, we have designed the *Bank Street Ready-to-Read* series in three levels to accommodate the individual stages of reading readiness of children ages four through eight.

○ *Level 1:* GETTING READY TO READ—read-alouds for children who are taking their first steps toward reading.

● *Level 2:* READING TOGETHER—for children who are just beginning to read by themselves but may need a little help.

○ *Level 3:* I CAN READ IT MYSELF—for children who can read independently.

Our three levels make it easy to select the books most appropriate for a child's development and enable him or her to grow with the series step by step. The *Bank Street Ready-to-Read* books also overlap and reinforce each other, further encouraging the reading process.

We feel that making reading fun and enjoyable is the single most important thing that you can do to help children become good readers. And we hope you'll be a part of Bank Street's long tradition of learning through sharing.

The Bank Street College of Education

To Glo and Bucky
—J.O.
To Luke
—A.M.

THE CHRISTMAS WITCH

A Bantam Book/November 1993

Published by Bantam Doubleday Dell Books for Young Readers,
a division of Bantam Doubleday Dell Publishing Group, Inc.
1540 Broadway, New York, New York 10036

Series graphic design by Alex Jay/Studio J

Special thanks to James A. Levine, Betsy Gould,
and Diane Arico.

The trademarks "Bantam Books" and the portrayal of a rooster
are registered in the U.S. Patent and Trademark Office and in
other countries. Marca Registrada.

Library of Congress Cataloging-in-Publication Data
Oppenheim, Joanne.
The Christmas Witch / retold by Joanne Oppenheim ;
illustrated by Annie Mitra.
p.   cm.—(Bank Street ready-to-read)
"A Byron Preiss book."
"A Bantam book."
Summary: Retells the traditional Italian tale
of the poor peasant woman who, long ago,
set out to find the Christ Child
and wanders to this day, carrying a sack of gifts
to give to good children at Christmas.
ISBN 0-553-09392-4.—ISBN 0-553-37187-8 (pbk.)
1. Befana (Legendary character)—Juvenile literature.
[1. Befana (Legendary character) 2. Folklore—Italy.
3. Christmas—Folklore.] I. Mitra, Annie, ill. II. Title. III. Series.
PZ8.1.057Ch   1993
398.21—dc20
[E]   92-562   CIP   AC

Published simultaneously in the United States and Canada

PRINTED IN THE UNITED STATES OF AMERICA

0 9 8 7 6 5 4 3

Bank Street Ready-to-Read™

The Christmas Witch

An Italian Legend

Retold by Joanne Oppenheim
Illustrated by Annie Mitra

A Byron Preiss Book

A BANTAM BOOK

Long ago, before the first Christmas,
there lived a very old woman called Befana.
Her tiny house stood in a small town
in a far corner of Italy.
Befana had no family or friends,
only a sleek black cat.
To fill her lonely days and nights,
Befana spent her time sweeping
and cooking
and sweeping some more.

While she cleaned,
Befana crooned little tunes.
Her singing was so awful that her neighbors
slammed their shutters tight.
"Such a wicked voice!" they complained.
"She sounds like a witch!"

"Stay away from that crazy old woman!"
people warned their children.
But the delicious smell of fresh cookies
often drifted from Befana's window,
tempting the children to go closer.

When old Befana came to the door
with her broom and black cat,
the children ran away screaming.
"Watch out for the witch!"

Befana did look like a witch.
She always wore black.
She never smiled at anyone.
She shook her broom at the children,
then went back to cooking and cleaning.

Early one evening,
Befana cleaned her whole house.
Then she went outside to sweep.
There in the evening sky
she saw the most amazing star.
It dazzled her eyes!

Befana stared up at the strange star.
It was the biggest, brightest star
she had ever seen in her whole long life.

When she went to bed that night,
Befana tossed and turned.
She tried sleeping on her left side
and then on her right.
She tried sleeping under her quilt
and on top of it.
No matter how she tried,
she could not sleep.
Nor could her poor cat.

Befana kept thinking
about the strange star.
Again and again she went to the window
to gaze at its dazzling light.
"What can it mean?" she said to her cat.

Since she couldn't sleep,
Befana began to cook and clean.
She was sweeping the stones
near her fireplace when she heard
the faraway sound of jingling bells.
At first she thought it might be
children playing tricks.

When she opened the door,
no one was there.
Yet the singing sound of bells
kept coming closer and closer.

Soon she saw a most remarkable sight.
There on the winding road came
an amazing procession of travelers.
Some were on foot carrying
flaming lights.

Others rode elephants, horses,
or tall, swaying camels with jingling bells.
Befana could not believe her poor old eyes.
Never in her long life
had she seen such a sight!

As the procession came closer,
Befana saw three kings
dressed in beautiful robes
the colors of jewels.
One wore ruby red.
One wore emerald green.
A third wore a robe of sapphire blue
shimmering with diamonds and pearls.

On their heads, golden crowns
glittered with jewels.
Befana was amazed when the procession
stopped at her tiny house.

But when the three kings
got off their camels
and came toward her,
Befana was frightened.
She started to run inside.
"Do not run away, my good woman,"
called one of the kings.
"We mean you no harm."

Befana's broom shook in her hand.
"Have you seen the star?"
asked the second king, pointing to the sky.
Befana nodded her head yes.
"We are following that star
to Bethlehem," he said.

"Is this the road to Bethlehem?"
asked the third king.
Befana did not know.
"I have never heard of Bethlehem,"
she said.
"Why do you want to go there?"

"My good woman," said the first king,
"have you not heard of the miracle?
We are bringing gifts to the Christ Child
who is born in Bethlehem."
"Come with us!" said the second king.

"I am just a poor old woman," answered Befana. "I have no gifts to bring the Child."

25

"That does not matter,"
the first king told her.
"He is here to make a better world
for rich and poor,
for young and old,
for all of us.
Like that star, He brings
new light to the world."

"And we must follow that star
to find Him," said the second king.
"But we must go now before we lose
sight of it," the third king said.
"Won't you come with us?"

Poor Befana could not make up her mind.
"Should I go or not?" she wondered.
"I have never been away
from my little town.
How can a poor old woman like me
travel with kings?
And who will keep my little house clean?"

Finally Befana looked up at the three kings.
"I can't go now," she said.
"Maybe I will follow you later."

And so Befana began sweeping
and cleaning
and sweeping some more.
She was still sweeping
as the kings on their camels
rode out of sight.

As she worked, Befana thought about
the Child who had been born
under that strange and dazzling star.
She wanted to see Him.
But how could she go without gifts?

31

"Maybe I can make some gifts,"
Befana said to her cat.
So she began sifting and stirring
her most delicious ginger cookies.
While they were baking, she sewed
a soft doll for the Christ Child.
As she worked, she crooned so loudly
that shutters slammed all over town.

When she was done,
Befana packed up the doll and cookies.
With her cat and her broom,
she set out for Bethlehem.

At first she followed the road
the three kings had taken.
She searched the sky for the glittering star
that would show her the way to Bethlehem.

But then the sky filled
with a shower of heavenly lights.
And a choir of angels sang . . .

JOY TO THE WORLD!
THE CHILD IS BORN!
GLORY TO GOD!
PEACE ON EARTH!
GOOD WILL TO ALL!

Befana could not find the one dazzling star
that would lead her to Bethlehem.
For now the sky shimmered
with so many stars
that the poor old woman did not know
which way to go.

She began running faster
and faster
and faster until . . .

Befana was flying!

All night Befana kept flying
over cities and towns,
over mountains and valleys,
over lakes and rivers,
over land and sea.

She kept searching and searching
for the dazzling star
and for the newborn Child
who lay beneath it.

Poor Befana never found her way to
Bethlehem that first Christmas.
But she never gave up trying.

Every year at Christmastime
Befana stops her sweeping.
She takes her broom and her cat
and flies all over Italy
searching for the Christ Child.

She flies from house to house
with her basket of toys and treats,
searching and searching
for the miracle she missed.

46

She slides down each chimney
with her cat and her broom,
leaving delicious cookies and small toys
for every sleeping child.
She never gives up hope that one day
she will find the Christ Child!

And every year,
in every far corner of Italy,
children still watch and wait for Befana—
the good Christmas Witch.

48